Mostly Ghostly 8

Don't Close Your Eyes!

Experience all the chills
of the Mostly Ghostly series!

Mostly Ghostly 8

Don't Close Your Eyes!

R.L. STINE

DELACORTE PRESS
A PARACHUTE PRESS BOOK

Published by Delacorte Press
an imprint of Random House Children's Books
a division of Random House, Inc.
New York

DELACORTE PRESS and colophon are registered trademarks of
Random House, Inc.

www.randomhouse.com/kids

Educators and librarians, for a variety of teaching tools, visit us at
www.randomhouse.com/teachers

B+T 8.99 1/06

Library of Congress Cataloging-in-Publication Data
Stine, R.L.
Don't close your eyes / R.L. Stine.—1st ed.
p. cm. — (Mostly ghostly)
"A Parachute Press Book."
Summary: Max already shares his house with two young ghosts
that only he can see, but things get really bad when an evil ghost
decides to share his body.
ISBN 0-385-74695-4 (hardcover)
ISBN 0-385-90933-0 (Gibraltar lib. bdg.)
[1. Ghosts—Fiction. 2. Horror stories.] I. Title.
II. Series: Stine, R.L. Mostly ghostly.
PZ7.S86037Dj 2006
[Fic] — dc22
2005014782

Printed in the United States of America

10 9 8 7 6 5 4 3 2 1

First Edition

TRACI WAYNE AND I sat across from each other at my kitchen table. Her math homework was spread out in front of me.

"Would you like me to show you how to do this equation?" I asked.

She glanced up from her *Teen People* magazine. "Max, couldn't you just *do* it for me? I have to catch up on my reading."

"Uh . . . yeah, sure," I muttered.

Yawning, I lowered my head to the page and started to scribble numbers and letters. My eyes were watering. I tried to blink them dry. I yawned again.

"Don't yawn so loud," Traci said. "How do you expect me to read?"

My eyelids drooped. They each weighed about a hundred pounds. I had to lift them up with my fingers.

I messed up the equation. I started to erase.

This doesn't sound normal, does it? This doesn't sound like Max Doyle, boy genius, the kid everyone in class calls Brainimon.

Well, it wasn't a normal afternoon. I wasn't feeling like myself at all. And I can tell you why—I hadn't slept in more than forty-eight hours.

Don't ever try staying awake for two whole days and nights. Your eyeballs burn. Your head feels like a granite boulder. And it feels as if your tongue is growing fur!

Normally, I'd be so excited to have Traci Wayne in my house, I'd do cartwheels or something. I admit it. I have a huge crush on Traci.

Whenever I see her, my heart starts to pound a hip-hop rhythm, my mouth goes as dry as talcum powder, and my knees knock together like bongos.

Traci once put her hand on my shoulder, and it gave me hiccups for three weeks.

That's true love, right?

Traci usually ignores me. It's because we're in different groups at school. She's in the way cool group. And I'm in the bottom feeders group.

My friend Aaron and I are the only ones in our group. And we're not quite sure how we got there. But we know there's no way out.

So when Traci comes over to my house, it's a

big-deal thing. Even if all she wants is for me to do her math homework while she reads *Teen People*.

But tonight, yawn, yawn.

All I wanted was to put my head down and go to sleep.

But I couldn't. I had to stay awake—maybe *forever*.

I'm not joking. See, I'm a normal sixth grader. But I have a problem. I have two ghosts living in my house.

Nicky and Tara Roland are about my age. They used to live here before my family moved in. Now they're back, and they don't know how they became ghosts.

They pop in and out all the time. And they're *my* problem—because I'm the only one who can see or hear them.

Lucky me, right?

Nicky and Tara are the reason I may never sleep again.

Yawn. If only I could stop yawning. And keep my eyelids from drooping . . . drooping.

"Max! What are you *doing*?" Traci's cry brought me back to life.

I blinked at her. "Huh?"

She pointed at my equations. "You're writing on the table, not on the paper!"

3

Blinking hard, I glanced down. She was right. I'd scribbled all over the kitchen table.

"Uh . . . just making some notes," I said. "I didn't want to mess up your notebook paper."

"Could you hurry up and finish?" Traci asked. "I'm getting kinda bored."

"No problem," I said. I turned back to the equation. But after a few seconds, my eyelids felt heavy . . . heavy. . . . I couldn't keep them open. I felt myself drifting . . . drifting into sleep.

"Whoa!" I let out a cry as cold water splashed over my head.

I looked up to see Tara tipping a bottle of water over me. "No sleeping, Max," she said. "You know you have to stay awake."

Of course, Traci couldn't hear or see Tara. All Traci could see was the water bottle floating over my head.

"Max!" she gasped. "That water—"

I reached up and pulled the bottle down to the table. "Did you miss science class last week?" I asked. "We learned that water *floats*."

I know. It didn't make sense. But I was too sleepy to think of a better excuse.

I went back to work on the equations. But I was yawning so loudly, I couldn't hear myself think.

How did this happen to me?

Why have I been awake for forty-eight hours?

And why will I maybe have to stay awake for the *rest of my life*?

Well, it's a long, frightening story. It all started two days before, with Tara innocently reading a book. . . .

2

Two days ago, I was sitting in front of my computer. It was after dinner and I was messaging my friend Aaron.

We're best friends, but we don't see each other very much. That's because Aaron is grounded for life. Actually, he's grounded for *three* lifetimes. And he had just IM'd me that he was grounded again.

> **BRAINIMON1:** Why are U grounded?
>
> **AARONDOG:** For doing a simple magic trick.
>
> **BRAINIMON1:** Since when r u into magic? I'm the 1 who does magic tricks!
>
> **AARONDOG:** It was an ez trick I showed my sister.
>
> **BRAINIMON1:** What trick?
>
> **AARONDOG:** I showed her how to turn her homework into confetti.
>
> **BRAINIMON1:** Nice trick.
>
> **AARONDOG:** She's still crying. And I'm grounded again.

BRAINIMON1: So we can't have our Stargate SG-1 club meeting again?

AARONDOG: We can have it in about 10 years.

I started to reply to Aaron. But I stopped when Nicky and Tara flashed into my room.

They appear and disappear without warning. Sometimes they fade away slowly and disappear for days at a time. They can't control it. Nicky says that's one of the hardest parts about being a ghost.

Tara says the *hardest* part is having to talk to *me* all the time!

I think she meant that as a joke.

They are both tall and thin. Serious-looking kids. Nicky is eleven, and Tara is nine. She has dark eyes and straight dark hair down to her shoulders. Nicky's hair and eyes are dark too. Tara always wears dangling plastic earrings, and she usually has a floppy red hat on her head.

Nicky dropped down onto the edge of my bed, his hands in his pockets. Tara carried an enormous book in both hands. It was opened to somewhere in the middle. She read it as she walked across the room.

"Is that a dictionary?" I asked.

She shook her head and stood in front of me, reading silently.

"It's another ghost book," Nicky said. "Another book about the supernatural world. Tara won't give up."

I turned my desk chair to face him. "Give up?"

"She keeps reading these ancient books," Nicky said. "She thinks maybe she'll find a clue that will help us return to life."

Tara raised her eyes. "Nicky and I don't want to be ghosts for the rest of our lives," she said. She shuddered. "Just reading about these old ghosts gives me the creeps. I don't want to turn into some evil *thing*."

"Too late. You already are!" Nicky said.

Tara stuck her tongue out at him and made a loud spitting noise.

He spit back at her.

She spit even louder and longer.

Gross! I had to stop it. Sometimes their spitting contests went on for an hour!

"Where did you get that huge book?" I asked Tara.

"I borrowed it from some library," Tara replied.

"You mean you *stole* it?" I asked.

"Well, I can't exactly get a library card, can I?" Tara snapped. "When is the last time an invisible person got a library card?"

"You don't have to bite my head off," I said. "I only asked a question."

"See? She *has* become an evil thing!" Nicky said.

Tara sighed. "I'm just worried, that's all. I keep reading book after book. But none of them has anything that might help Nicky and me. They're just filled with evil ghosts and horrible spells and . . . no clue. Just no clue about how a ghost can come back to life for real."

She turned the page. "It's all so awful and frightening," she said. "Look at this one. A ghost called Inkweed. Wow. He was totally evil."

"Let me see it," Nicky said. He made a grab for the book.

Tara swung it away from him. "Hey—I'm reading it!"

Nicky grabbed again, and the big book fell out of Tara's hands.

It hit the floor with a hard *thud*.

Tara bent to pick it up—then stopped. "Oh no," she murmured. She stumbled back.

"What's your problem?" Nicky asked.

I stared down at the open pages. It took a few seconds for my eyes to focus. Then I gasped when I saw what had frightened Tara.

The letters on the pages—the ancient black type, the words—they were all *moving*! Sliding over the yellowed pages, moving into the center of the book.

3

ALL THREE OF US stared down at the open book on the floor, frozen in shock.

The words written about the evil ghost Inkweed slid quickly to the middle and formed a black puddle of ink. The puddle spread silently over the book, growing wider and deeper.

"This is *crazy!*" I cried.

All three of us gasped as the ink puddle began to rise off the book. It lifted itself up as if it was alive! A living ink creature.

"Inkweed is alive!" Tara screamed. Then she and Nicky flickered and faded. The shock was taking away their energy force.

But I could see the horror on their faces as the ink blob floated up into the air. It made a wet slapping sound as it settled against the bedroom wall. Then it began to shift and spread.

"Stop it! We have to *stop* it!" Tara screamed.

Nicky flickered in and out like a firefly. "H-how?" he stammered.

I jumped up from my desk chair and started

backing up, moving away from the shadowy ink blob as it spread over my wall.

It continued to spread, and then it pulled itself into a new shape. Slowly, slowly, it started to form a black, inky figure—the silhouette of a man!

"Is it . . . is it *Inkweed*?" Tara choked out.

Before anyone could answer, the inky shadow pulled off the wall—and floated over my head.

I ducked.

I tried to dodge it.

But it settled over me. Hot and wet. Like someone dropping a heavy wet bath towel over me.

I couldn't move. I couldn't see.

The dark shadow held me in place. It wrapped around me. My skin prickled under the hot wetness of it. Shiver after shiver rolled down my body.

I tried to cry out, but my voice was muffled under the thick, black shadow.

The shadow grew heavier. I bent over. Dropped to my knees under its weight.

I tried to scream. I tried to thrash my arms and duck my head to escape the terrifying blanket.

But I was frozen beneath it.

And then I felt it shift and start to settle. It was settling over me. No. Not settling.

Sinking.

Sinking into me!

Sinking into my skin. Into my *brain*!

My arms jerked. My head was flung back as if someone had slugged me.

I toppled over. My head hit the floor.

I felt as if I was swimming in blackness. Deep underwater in a freezing black pond. I felt the wet currents splashing inside me, one after the other.

And then I was back on my feet. Still squinting through a thick curtain of gray. Still shivering. Shaking my head, trying to shake the dark clouds away.

"Max!" Tara cried. Her shout sounded very far away. "Max! Are you okay?"

"Oh, wow." I heard Nicky's voice somewhere on the other side of the black curtain. "Max, you're covered in black ink. You're dripping!"

"Never mind that!" I shouted, surprised to hear my normal voice. "It's *inside* me! I can feel it!"

"Inkweed?" Nicky asked. "Is it Inkweed?"

The dark curtain lifted a little. I could see the two ghosts gaping at me in horror.

"I don't know what it is," I said. "But I can feel it inside my body! Inside my *head*!"

"Oh no. Oh no," Tara moaned, tugging her hat down over her ears.

"*Do* something!" I screamed. "Pick up the book! Hurry! You've got to help me. What does it say to do?"

4

THEY BOTH STARED AT me. I could feel the ink running down my face. I used my T-shirt sleeve to wipe it away from my eyes.

"The book," I said, pointing. "Hurry. Please."

Nicky reached down and hoisted the huge book up in both hands. "It's . . . it's blank," he said. "All the ink is gone."

Tara took the book from him. She started flipping rapidly through the pages. "Gone," she muttered. "The words . . . they're all gone."

I felt Inkweed shift inside my head. It felt like a beanbag rolling around up there.

"Give that book to me!" I screamed. Tara gasped as I jerked the book from her hands.

"Max?" she cried. "What are you—"

I raised the book in front of me, held it high—and with a violent motion, ripped it in half. Grunting loudly, I ripped the ancient, crumbling pages, ripped them to shreds.

When I finished, I was panting hard. Shredded paper was piled ankle-deep around me.

Tara grabbed me by the shoulders. "Max—are you *crazy*? Why did you do that?"

It took me a long time to answer. I was gasping for breath. The room was spinning all around me.

"I . . . I didn't do it!" I finally cried. "*He* did it! *He* made me do it!"

"Inkweed?" Nicky asked. "Inkweed made you tear the book to pieces?"

I nodded. I could feel my throat tighten. My breath came out in hoarse wheezes. I don't think I've ever been that scared.

"I don't have control of my own body," I told them. "It's horrible. To be forced to do something you don't want to do. I'm not in control. *Please*—help me."

"Help you do *what*?" a voice called from my bedroom doorway.

I turned to see my older brother, Colin, standing there. I let out a groan. Even though we're brothers, Colin is not exactly my best buddy.

I guess I just don't like Colin's favorite hobby, which is *torturing* me!

"Help you do *what*, Fat Face?" he said, stomping into my room.

"Don't call me Fat Face," I said.

"What else can I call you?" Colin replied. "I can't call you *Thin* Face, can I? Because—let's be real here—you have the fattest face in our family."

"I'm kinda busy," I said. "Why don't you go

14

back to your room and do some push-ups or sit-ups or whatever you do for fun?"

He rolled his eyes. "I already did one hundred of each," he said. "My after-dinner workout. I always do one hundred push-ups and one hundred sit-ups to warm up for my late-night workout."

Colin, you see, is perfect.

"You should work out," Colin said, grabbing my stomach and pinching it as hard as he could. "Then you wouldn't go around looking like a pig on steroids."

He let go of me. Then he picked something gross out of his nose and wiped it on my bedspread.

Nicky and Tara watched the whole scene from the side of the room. Of course, Colin couldn't see them. "Don't let him get away with that, Max," Tara said.

"What can I do?" I asked her.

"What can you do about what?" Colin asked. "That glob of ugly fat above your neck?"

"I—I—I—" I started to stammer. I was too scared and upset to deal with Colin.

Colin kicked at the pile of shredded paper on the floor. "Hey, Max, why did you tear up this old book?"

"Uh . . . well . . . I was finished with it," I said.

Colin stared at me. Slowly, his grin faded. His expression turned serious. "Maxie, you—you're shaking. And you are pale white. Are you okay?"

"Not really," I muttered.

"Tell Colin to leave," Tara said.

"Yeah. Tell him to beat it," Nicky said.

"*You* tell him!" I said.

Colin squinted harder at me. "Me? Tell who what?" Colin asked. "Are you totally losing it?"

"Maybe," I said. I felt Inkweed move around in my chest. I started to shiver even harder.

Colin put a hand on my shoulder. "Hey, I'm your big bro, right?"

I nodded. I waited for the usual punch in the gut, but it didn't come.

"Well, you can tell me what the problem is." He brushed back my hair. "I know sometimes I'm a little rough on you. I mean, sometimes I like to punch you and hurt you and make you cry. But that's just for fun. That's just my nature."

"Yeah," I said. I didn't know what else to say.

"But I can see you're messed up," Colin said, sliding his heavy arm around my trembling shoulders. "You can tell me what the problem is, Max. I can be a good listener. Really. Especially if it's important to my little bro."

I stared at him. "Promise you won't laugh at me the way you always do?"

He crossed his heart with two fingers. "No way would I laugh at you," he said. "I'm here to help you. No lie."

I believed him. I was so desperate, so terrified, I believed him.

I glanced to the side of the room. But Nicky and Tara had disappeared.

I turned back to Colin. "That old book was filled with ghost stories," I told him. "It had a story in it about an evil ghost named Inkweed."

"Sure it wasn't *Stink*weed?" Colin asked, sniffing my armpit.

"Please don't try to make jokes," I said. "Come on. You promised you wouldn't laugh at me."

He made a zipping motion over his lips.

"The book fell on the floor," I continued. "And something *horrible* happened. The words started to move. The ink all slid together. It became a big black puddle."

Colin shut his eyes and scrunched up his face. I couldn't tell what that meant.

"The puddle floated off the book and formed the shape of a man," I said, my voice shaking. "Inkweed. Inkweed lifted off the book and . . . and . . ."

It was so frightening, it was hard to say. "And Inkweed floated into me," I finally choked out.

"I . . . I'm in so much trouble, Colin," I said. "That evil ghost—he's inside me. He can control me. I . . . I don't know what to do."

I was trembling hard now. I couldn't say another word.

Colin opened his eyes. He slid his arm around my shoulder again. "Hey, no problem, Max," he said softly. "Good you confided in your older bro. I know how to get Inkweed out."

My mouth dropped open. "You *do*?"

5

"**YEAH. NO PROBLEM,**" **COLIN** said. "Here. Watch."

He pulled back his arm and let me have it—a solid punch to the soft part of my stomach.

"*Urrrrrk.*" A sound escaped my throat that I'd never heard before.

I doubled over in agony, holding my stomach. "Urrrk urrrk urrrk," I kept honking. I struggled to breathe.

Colin stood watching me with his hands at his waist. "Did the nasty ghost come out?" he asked.

"The only thing . . . that came out . . . was . . . my dinner," I groaned.

It took a long time to stand up straight. When I did, I glared at Colin angrily. "Hey—you said you wouldn't laugh at me."

He tossed back his head and laughed for about five minutes.

"Maxie, don't you ever get tired of making up these lame ghost stories?" he asked. "Inkweed!

Stinkweed! You're too old for that dumb stuff! Did you really think I'd believe you?"

"Yes," I said, shaking a fist at him. "Yes. I confided in you, Colin. I trusted you because . . . because . . ."

I didn't know why.

"Okay, okay," Colin said, raising both hands as if surrendering. "Here's another idea."

He disappeared into the hallway for a few seconds. When he returned, he had three fat rolls of toilet paper in his hands. He grabbed me around the waist, held me tight, and started wrapping toilet paper around my chest.

"Stop it!" I shouted. "What are you doing?"

"Making you a straitjacket," he said. "Because you're nuts!"

"Stop it! Let go of me!" I tried to squirm away, but he was too strong.

Colin snickered. "Dad just got back from the outlet store. He bought three cases of toilet paper. So I'm putting it to good use."

He wrapped it around my chest, my waist, my arms. I slumped in place and didn't try to struggle. What was the point?

"This looks good on you, Maxie," he said, wrapping it around my head. "A cool new look."

"Mmmmmff mmmmmfff," I said.

"Maybe this is how mummies felt," he said. "Of course, they were dead first."

He wrapped a while longer. I didn't move or struggle. It was better than being punched in the stomach.

Mom usually tries to make Colin stop torturing me, but Dad thinks he's a riot. Dad thinks everything Colin does is wonderful. He says Colin isn't mean to me. He's only trying to make a man out of me.

"Hey, Freak Face, I'm telling Dad you're wasting good toilet paper," Colin said. I heard him walk out of my room giggling.

As soon as he was gone, I struggled out of the paper cocoon. My heart was pounding, and I felt dizzy.

I searched for Nicky and Tara. No sign of them.

Maybe I'll try to do some homework, I decided. I'll force myself to work so I won't be able to think about what just happened.

I pulled out my science notebook. I had a worksheet to fill in. I spread it out on my desk. Then I searched my drawer for a pencil.

The worksheet had about twenty elements to identify. Easy stuff. I could do it with my eyes closed.

I leaned over the paper and started to write.

Whoa. Wait.

I stopped and stared at the page. What were those black spots?

I pushed my finger into one. Wet.

Black ink. Several black ink spots on the page. Another one dropped near my finger.

"Oh nooooo," I moaned.

The black ink was dripping from my nose.

6

HOLDING MY NOSE, I jumped up from the desk. I staggered across the room and grabbed up big wads of toilet paper off the floor.

I jammed the toilet paper up my nose.

The black ink dripped from my nose for another minute or two. I wadded the toilet paper tighter. Finally, it stopped.

Breathing hard, I dropped onto the edge of my bed.

What am I going to do? I let out a moan.

I had never felt so weird or so frightened. I could feel the evil ghost moving inside me . . . inside my head. Now it felt like a snake slithering around in my skull.

Even though the dripping had stopped, I held the wadded-up paper to my nose. Maybe I should tell Mom and Dad what happened, I thought.

But—no. I'd told them too many ghost stories.

All true. But my parents thought I made them up. They thought I had a thing about ghosts. And a wild imagination.

No way would they believe me about Inkweed.

I gasped when I saw Mom poke her head into my room. "Max? What are you doing?" she asked, gaping at the tall pile of toilet paper on the floor. "What is this mess?"

"Uh . . . it's an art thing," I said. "I'm making papier-mâché. For a sculpture I'm doing of you. For Mother's Day."

She squinted at me. "But Mother's Day is six months away."

"It takes a long time to dry," I said.

Mom stared at the toilet paper for a long moment. Then she disappeared down the hall.

"Good one, Max." Nicky slapped me on the back.

"Yeah. Fast thinking," Tara said, suddenly reappearing beside her brother.

"I *have* to think fast—ever since you two arrived," I grumbled. "But this is the worst. Look what you've *done* to me!"

"We can deal with it," Nicky said.

"There has to be a way to get Inkweed out of you," Tara said. She gave me a push toward my computer. "Google him, Max. Hurry."

I blinked. I felt the snake slither to the front of my head.

"Google Inkweed," Tara said. "Let's see what we can find out about this ghost."

"Okay," I said. I felt the snake crawl behind

my forehead to the back of my skull, then down the back of my neck.

Somehow I kept myself from screaming.

I sat in front of the keyboard. I raised my hands to the keys.

And felt myself lose control.

As I started to type, I realized I wasn't the one typing. My fingers hit the keys. But someone else was telling them what to write. . . .

"I know who you are, Nicky and Tara Roland. As soon as I escape this body, I will cover all three of you in my inky blackness. Once this boy's body falls asleep, I come alive! And all three of you will sleep forever!"

My hands dropped heavily to my sides. I was gasping for breath, my chest heaving.

"I . . . I didn't write that!" I cried.

Nicky and Tara leaned over me, staring at the screen.

"I didn't type that," I gasped. "Inkweed made my fingers move."

My whole body shuddered. "I . . . I don't have control of my own hands." I stared at the words on the monitor. But I was too frightened to focus. They were a blur to me.

"What are we going to do?" I cried.

Tara put a hand on my shoulder. "We have to keep you awake, Max. We can't let you fall asleep until we find a way to send Inkweed back where he came from."

"I have to stay awake?" I said in a trembling voice. "But . . . it's late. I'm toast. I'm really tired."

"Come on, dude," Nicky said. "No sleep tonight. We'll play some video games."

"Yeah. I'll get some nacho chips and drinks downstairs," Tara said. "We'll pretend it's an all-night party."

"Just don't fall asleep, Max." Nicky stared hard at me. "You can't fall asleep until we figure out how to get rid of Inkweed."

"Right," Tara said. She clutched my shoulders. "Max, if you fall asleep, we're all doomed."

7

I STAGGERED DOWN TO breakfast a little after seven-thirty.

Mom, Dad, and Colin were already at the table. Mom glanced up from her coffee mug. "You look tired this morning, Max," she said.

Well, duh. Of *course* I looked tired. I was up all night playing video games. I watched the sun come up.

Colin scooped cereal into his mouth, making loud slurping and chewing noises.

Dad raised a grapefruit half and squeezed the juice into his open mouth. He never eats his grapefruit. He just squeezes it until it looks like a limp rag.

Colin burped really loudly.

"Stop it, please," Mom said softly, lowering her coffee mug.

"Max taught me how to do that," Colin said.

Yawning, I plopped down beside Colin. I was in no mood for his dumb jokes.

27

Dad finished squeezing his grapefruit and tossed it across the room, into the sink. "Two points!" he shouted.

My dad is a big, loud, red-faced Mack truck of a guy. He's a pretty good dad. But he's huge, and he thinks he's tough. And he thinks I should be macho and tough like Colin and him.

Fat chance.

I yawned again. My eyelids felt heavy. I reached for the salt to sprinkle on my scrambled eggs.

"Are you bringing your phys ed grade up?" Dad asked me.

"Huh?" I blinked at him.

"Max, you promised you'd try out for the swim team to impress your coach. Remember?"

I rolled my eyes. "Dad, I get all A's. The kids call me Brainimon. They all call me to help them with their homework because I'm the class brain. And all you care about is my C in phys ed."

Dad pulled up his shirt sleeve and flexed his biceps in my face. When he flexed his right bicep muscle, it made his dragon tattoo appear to spit red flames.

"There's nothing more important in life than being fit," Dad said. He picked up another grapefruit half and squeezed it into his mouth until it was dry. Pulp ran down his chin.

He waved the limp grapefruit rind in my face. "Can *you* do that?"

"Uh . . . I can do it with a grape!" I said.

It was a joke, but no one laughed.

"I can do it with Max's head," Colin said.

Dad grinned at him. "Colin, you always set a good example for Max," he said.

"I know," Colin said. He turned to me. "There's something on the back of your pants, Max. Stand up."

"Excuse me?" Normally, I wouldn't have fallen for Colin's dumb trick. But I was so tired, I obeyed. I stood up.

"No, I was wrong," Colin said. "No problem."

I didn't see him slip my plate of scrambled eggs onto my chair. So I plopped down and sat on my eggs.

Dad tossed back his head and roared with laughter. Colin joined him.

"Maxie, don't play with your food," Mom said.

I opened my mouth to protest. But something terrible happened.

I felt it rise from my chest . . . and into my throat.

And then it spewed from my open mouth. A gusher of thick black ink.

Like a strong spray from a garden hose, it doused the table.

I struggled to close my jaw. But the force of the spray kept my mouth open wide.

The ink covered the table, splashed onto Mom, Dad, and Colin, and puddled on the floor.

"Stop it! Stop it!"

I heard their screams.

But I was helpless.

I couldn't stop.

8

DR. WELLES GRUNTED. HE pressed the stethoscope to my bare chest.

"*Yaaaiiii!*" I let out a cry.

"I keep it in the freezer," he said. "I like to see the look on people's faces."

He was joking. Dr. Welles has a good sense of humor. He's young and blond and good-looking. He looks more like a tennis player than a doctor.

But his smile quickly faded. He listened to my chest for a while. Then he had me lie down on my stomach on the examining table, and he listened to different parts of my back.

My eyelids drooped. They felt so heavy. Heavy.

"Hmmmm," the doctor said. "That's doctor talk for 'I don't know what's going on here.'"

"Don't fall asleep, Max," I heard a voice whisper. I glanced up to see Nicky and Tara standing by the examining table.

"Go away," I said.

"I can't," Dr. Welles replied. "This is my office."

31

"Your eyes were closing," Tara said. "Keep them open."

"We're watching you, Max," Nicky said.

"Don't watch me," I said.

"Then how can I examine you?" Dr. Welles asked.

"I wasn't talking to you," I said.

He squinted at me.

"This is a waste of time," Tara said. "We already know what the problem is. Let's get out of here." She tugged at my arm.

"Put your arm down, please," the doctor said.

Tara pulled my arm again. "Come on. Tell him you're in a hurry."

"Put your arm down, please," Dr. Welles repeated.

"Uh . . . just exercising," I said. I jerked my arm away from Tara and almost fell off the examining table.

Dr. Welles pulled me up to a sitting position. "Let's take a good look at your throat."

He raised a flat, wooden tongue depressor about the size of a yardstick and jammed it onto my tongue. Then he shined a bright light down my throat.

"Hey, I can see China!" he said. I guess that was one of his standard jokes.

"He isn't going to find Inkweed that way," Tara said.

"Stay awake, Max," Nicky warned. "Don't drift off."

How could I fall asleep with a light down my throat?

Dr. Welles shook his head. He pulled the light from my mouth. Then he aimed it into my eyes. "Max, did you get much sleep last night?" he asked.

I shook my head. "Not much."

I can't fall asleep because an evil ghost will pour out of my body and destroy us.

"Well, put your shirt back on," Dr. Welles said. He walked to his desk and started scribbling in a notebook.

A few minutes later, my mom came in to get the report.

"I didn't see anything unusual," Dr. Welles said, brushing back his blond hair. "It must have been something he ate."

Something I ate?

"He seems okay now," the doctor continued. "Maybe he should stay home today and sleep."

"No way!" Nicky and Tara both screamed.

"Shut up!" I said.

Mom and Dr. Welles both stared at me. "Did you just tell me to shut up?" he asked.

"Uh . . . shut up that cabinet over there," I said, pointing. "Before the tongue depressors start falling out."

*   *   *

33

A short while later, Mom led me out to the parking lot. She stopped before we climbed into the car. "Something you ate made you spew up all that black ink?"

"Uh . . . I had writer's block last night," I said. "Maybe I just came unblocked!"

I know. I know. It didn't make any sense.

But I was too sleepy to think of a better explanation.

I'd been awake for more than twenty-six hours. My ears rang. My skin itched. Even my *hair* felt heavy!

I lowered my gaze. The bright sunlight hurt my eyes.

The thing inside me doesn't like light, I realized. I felt it slithering around behind my forehead.

I shuddered. I suddenly felt cold all over.

Inkweed said he'd put me to sleep forever!

And as soon as I fell asleep . . .

Mom drove home. She kept glancing over at me. "Maxie, are you feeling okay?" She asked it about a dozen times.

I guess she could see I couldn't stop shivering.

"Yeah. I'm okay," I answered each time.

"I will cover all three of you in my inky blackness. All three of you will sleep forever!"

I'm okay as long as I don't close my eyes for the rest of my life!

34

We drove the rest of the way home in silence. Mom pulled the car into the driveway. "Max, I have to go to work now," Mom said. "I want you to go right upstairs and take a nap, okay? The doctor said you should get some rest."

"Yeah, sure," I said.

A nap sounded so sweet. I could *feel* the soft pillow against my face.

I watched Mom back out of the drive and pull away.

I reached for the front door. My eyes started to close.

I sat down and began to fall asleep on the front stoop.

"What do you think you're doing?" a voice cried.

Nicky and Tara pulled me off the steps.

"I . . . I . . ." I was too sleepy to form words.

"Let's go," Tara said, tugging me toward the street. "We think we know someone who can help."

9

WE WALKED THREE OR four blocks. I had to keep my eyes half-shut because the sunlight made them burn.

We hurried past my school. I tried to hide behind hedges so no one could look out a window and see me.

I was missing a science test. But it was just as well. I knew I'd only fall asleep at my desk.

"Where are you taking me?" I asked my two ghost friends.

"Over there." They both pointed.

Behind a row of tangled trees, I saw a sloping front yard, choked with weeds. And at the top of the hill—half-hidden by tall evergreen shrubs—stood a small gray house.

"We're going to that house?" I asked. "Who lives there?"

"No one," Nicky replied. "It isn't a house. See?"

As we walked closer, I saw the small wooden sign near the gravel driveway. In black stenciled letters, it read LIBRARY OF THE SPIRITUAL WORLD.

Twigs and dried weeds crackled under my shoes as we made our way up the sloping front lawn. I had to kick away clumps of dead brown leaves.

The sunlight disappeared as we stepped under the old trees. A cool wind ruffled my T-shirt. The house stood dark and silent at the top. I didn't see any signs of life.

We stepped into the deep shadow of the old house. "Why are we coming here?" I asked.

"This is where I got that book," Tara said. "Maybe they have another copy of it."

"Or maybe they know something about Inkweed," Nicky said.

He pushed open the heavy front door. The wood was warped. It squealed as the door slid open.

Dark inside. A musty smell floated over us, dry and kind of sour.

I followed them in. The floorboards creaked under my shoes. We made our way along a long narrow hall. Thick tangles of cobweb reached down from the low ceiling.

"It's not like a library. More like a haunted house," I whispered.

"Don't say that," Nicky said. "One evil ghost is enough."

I yawned. The air inside was hot and musty. Making me sleepy.

I felt Inkweed slide around my bones. That woke me up in a hurry!

We stepped into a big circular room with bookshelves all around from floor to ceiling. The room was dimly lit. But I could see that all the books looked ancient.

A long wooden desk piled high with books and papers stood at the far wall. Standing behind the desk was a pleasant-looking young woman with bright coppery hair and blue eyes. She wore jeans and a black sweater with a pair of gold cat's eyes on the front.

"That's Ms. Park, the librarian," Tara said. "Go up to her, Max. She can't see Nicky and me. So you'll have to do all the talking."

Tara gave me a shove toward the librarian's desk. She shoved too hard. I stumbled into a table and knocked over a stack of books.

"Oh!" Ms. Park uttered a startled cry.

"Sorry," I said. I bent down to pick up the fallen books. They were heavy and old and smelled of dust and decay.

Would one of these books help me get rid of Inkweed?

"Didn't see that table," I said. "It snuck up on me."

She smiled at me. "It's kind of dark in here. My

dad likes it like that. He says it gives the place atmosphere. I think it's hard to look for books. But I can't argue with him."

I stepped up to the desk. "Hi, I'm Max," I said. "Max Doyle."

"I'm Sumner Park," she said. "I haven't seen you here before."

"Uh . . . no."

"Are you interested in ghosts and the spiritual world, Max?" she asked.

"Not really," I said.

"Stop stalling," Tara said sharply. "Go ahead and ask her about Inkweed."

"Don't rush me," I said.

Ms. Park's smile faded. "I didn't mean to rush you. We're open till eight tonight."

"Not you," I said.

She glanced over my shoulder. "Did someone come in with you?"

"No," I said.

"Well, can I help you with something, Max?"

"Yes," I said. "I . . . uh . . . well . . ."

"Spit it out," Tara said.

"Leave me alone," I told her.

Ms. Park squinted at me. "Are you joking? Did you *really* come in here to tell me to leave you alone?"

"N-no," I stammered. "It's not a joke. I came to ask you about a ghost. I thought maybe . . ."

"You want information about a ghost?" she asked. "Well, you've come to the right place." She waved her hand. "See all these books? They're all about ghosts."

"Good," I said. "I need help. I mean . . ."

"What ghost did you want to ask about, Max?" Ms. Park asked.

I took a deep breath. "Inkweed," I said.

Ms. Park gasped. She backed away from the desk. Her eyes grew wide and her expression became tense. "Inkweed?" she asked. "Why are you asking me about Inkweed?"

10

I COULDN'T TELL HER the truth. If I said I was possessed by Inkweed, she might throw me out. She looked so frightened.

"It's . . . uh . . . for a school project," I said. "I have to write a report."

That seemed to calm her down a little. She stepped back up to the desk. "Sorry I jumped like that," she said, brushing back her red hair. "My dad used to tell me stories about Inkweed when I was little. And they *terrified* me."

"I guess he's a pretty scary ghost," I said.

Ms. Park nodded. "My dad told me when Inkweed attacks, he can cover a person in darkness. Just spread a deep shadow over that person. And from then on, the poor victim is invisible. Too dark to be seen by the human eye."

I made a loud gulping sound. I didn't like that story.

"I remember another one," she said, shutting her eyes. "Inkweed can cover your whole body

41

with a thick layer of black ink. As thick as a blanket. And it can't be erased, or pulled off, or washed off. You become like an ink creature. And eventually you suffocate because the ink oozes into your nose and mouth."

"Nice," I said. I shuddered. "Those were the bedtime stories your dad told you?"

She nodded. "My dad is a famous storyteller. He travels around the country telling his ghost stories to kids."

"He . . . he likes to scare kids?" I asked.

"He loves to dream up stories," Ms. Park replied. She motioned around the room. "These books . . . Dad collected them all. To help him make up new stories."

I stared at the old books cramming the shelves. "And he knows all about Inkweed, huh?"

She nodded. "Yes, he can probably help you with your report. He's upstairs in the private reading room."

"Can we see him?" I asked.

She squinted at me. *"We?"*

"I mean *me*," I said. I was so sleepy, I didn't know *what* I was saying!

"Have a seat over there," Ms. Park said. She pointed to a chair at a table. "I'll go upstairs and ask him if he'll see you."

"Thanks," I said. Yawning, I dropped into the chair.

I stretched my neck, trying to wake up a little. I yawned again.

It was hot in the library. Hot and silent. My head suddenly felt as heavy as a boulder.

I tried to fight it. I really tried. But I couldn't keep my eyes open another second.

I lowered my head to the table.

So quietly . . . so silently . . .

I shut my eyes and felt myself drifting into a deep sleep.

11

"Owwwwww!"

I opened my mouth in a scream. Sharp, blinding pain stabbed the top of my head.

My eyes shot open. "Hey—"

Tara had smashed a big book over my head.

"Sorry, Max," she said. "I had no choice."

"That book—!" Ms. Park cried, coming back into the room.

I turned and saw her pointing at me. "Max—that book! It fell on you from out of nowhere!"

I rubbed my head. "Uh . . . yeah, I know," I replied. "It's about lumberjacks. You know—*timberrrr!*"

I know. It didn't make any sense. I guess that's why Ms. Park kept staring at me.

"Max, what's that all over your face?" she asked. "It looks like ink."

"Oh, wow," I muttered.

"Inkweed started to escape from you," Nicky explained. "As soon as you closed your eyes, he started to ooze out."

44

I rubbed my cheeks. Inky wet.

"Uh . . . I guess my pen leaked!" I told the librarian.

I swallowed. My heart began to pound. Inkweed had started to make his escape. He had started to seep out of me.

I had to stay awake. But how? I could barely keep my eyes open, even after the hard smash on the head.

Ms. Park handed me a wad of tissues. I frantically wiped the ink off my face.

"Come with me," she said. "Dad said to bring you upstairs."

She led me up a creaky, narrow stairway. Nicky and Tara followed close behind. We entered a small low-ceilinged room crammed with books from floor to ceiling.

Ms. Park's father sat in a fat overstuffed armchair, a stack of books on a table at his side. He had a round red face, curly white hair, and bright blue eyes. He gave me a warm smile as I entered the room, and waved me into a folding chair across from him.

He wore an oversized brown cardigan sweater open over a black T-shirt, and baggy khakis, torn at one knee. He had a fat yellowed book open on his lap.

"So you're interested in folktales," he said. He had a deep, gravelly voice.

45

"Uh . . . well . . . n-no," I stammered.

He scratched his head of thick white hair. "I see. You're only interested in folktales about Inkweed."

I nodded. "Yes. Inkweed."

Mr. Park bit his bottom lip, studying me. "Well, he's an interesting ghost. Evil as they come."

"I know," I said. "I . . . uh . . . have one important question. For my school report."

He leaned closer. "And the question is?"

I took a deep breath. "If someone gets possessed by Inkweed," I said, "how do you get rid of him?"

"Get rid of him?" Mr. Park said. "That's *impossible*!"

12

I OPENED MY MOUTH in a loud gasp.

I felt Inkweed move inside my head. He slid from the back to my forehead. I could feel his heavy presence behind my eyes.

Mr. Park shut his eyes and rubbed his chin. "Let me think," he said. "How does the story go?"

He was silent for a long time.

I sucked in breath after breath, trying to calm down. But how could I? I wanted to scream at the top of my lungs. I wanted to scream for help.

"Somebody, help me! I've got this inky thing *inside me! Do something! Somebody—do something!"*

"Now I remember." Mr. Park's raspy voice broke into my panicked thoughts.

"You . . . r-remember?" I stammered.

He nodded. "It's impossible to get rid of Inkweed—*unless* you do one thing."

"Yes?" I cried eagerly. "One thing?"

"You must take Inkweed to the darkest place on the darkest night," Mr. Park said.

47

"The darkest place on the darkest night," I whispered to myself.

"Yes," the old storyteller said. "If you can keep him in darkness that's darker than *his* darkness, you will defeat him. He will disappear."

I stood there gazing into Mr. Park's face, thinking hard. I kept repeating the words he'd just said. Trying to make sense of them. Trying to understand . . .

Finally, I realized he was waiting for me to leave.

"Thank you very much," I said. "I think that will . . . uh . . . help my report a lot." I turned and started toward the stairway.

"Max, would you like to hear a story about a ghost named Turnip?" he called after me.

"No thanks," I said. "I—"

"They call him that because you never know where or when he'll turnip!" He laughed. "Get it?"

"Ha, ha," I laughed weakly. "That's a good one. Thanks again, Mr. Park." I gave him a wave and started down the stairs.

My legs were trembling. I could still feel Inkweed in my head. I couldn't wait to get out of that library.

Sumner Park wasn't at the front desk. I hurried away without saying goodbye.

I ran down the weed-choked front lawn, out

from under the shade of the old trees, and into the sunlight. Nicky and Tara followed me.

Breathing hard, I turned to them. "You heard what he said," I panted. "Now what?"

They stared at me without answering.

"How can we take Inkweed to the darkest place on the darkest night?" I asked. "What does that *mean*?"

13

NICKY SHRUGGED. HE SHOOK his head sadly.

"I don't have a clue," Tara said. "I'm sorry. It doesn't make any sense at all."

"I know," I said in a whisper. "I'm clueless too."

Tara grabbed my shoulder. "But we'll figure it out, Max. You just have to stay awake until we figure it out."

I yawned. "I'm trying," I said. "But it's hard. I'm so sleepy. . . ."

"I can't keep hitting you over the head with books," Tara said. "Your head will be as flat as a pancake! You've got to force yourself . . ."

She faded out before she could finish her sentence. Nicky faded too and then vanished from sight.

That happens to them a lot.

Sometimes when things get really intense, they use up all their spirit energy. And they disappear for a while.

So there I stood all alone. Thinking hard about what Mr. Park had said, I started to walk home. I was so sleepy, I walked right into a mailbox!

I turned to make sure no one had seen me. I glanced at my watch. Four in the afternoon.

I quickly did the math. That meant I'd been awake for thirty-three straight hours!

We had to figure out the darkest place on the darkest night, *fast*. I knew I couldn't fight off sleep much longer.

I was a block from home when I saw the Wilbur brothers standing on a corner, talking to some girls from my class. Billy and Willy Wilbur are the two worst kids at my school, Jefferson Elementary.

They are mean. They are loud. They think they are really tough dudes. They're just plain bad news.

I didn't want to run into them when I was only half-awake. I turned and tried to duck behind a row of bushes. But Willy Wilbur saw me and hurried to pull me over to them.

"Hey, Brainimon, whussup?" Willy asked.

"Whussup?" Billy repeated.

"Not much," I said.

The two girls giggled. They had strange smiles on their faces. Like they knew a joke that I didn't know.

"How's it going, Maxie?" Billy asked, also grinning.

"Okay," I said.

And before I could move, Willy had sneaked up behind me, grabbed my jeans, and pulled them down to my knees.

The Wilburs and the two girls burst out laughing. They laughed like it was the funniest thing they'd ever seen.

Billy banged me hard on the shoulder. "The girls bet us we couldn't de-pants you," he said. "That's a bet we had to win!"

The four of them laughed all over again.

I knew my face was bright red. I could feel it grow hot. These were two of the coolest girls in my class. And I was very upset. I didn't like being de-pantsed in front of them.

I bent to pull up my jeans. And as I did, I felt something like a ball of hot steam rise up from my chest.

Anger. A kind of red, raging anger I'd never felt before.

I felt it explode inside me.

I couldn't stop myself. I was no longer in control.

I whirled around blindly. The grass, the trees, the houses, the Wilburs, and the girls—all became a red blur in my eyes.

I started to spin . . . faster . . . faster . . . spinning like a tornado.

A fierce cry burst from my throat. A furious roar, more animal than human.

Out of control. I spun out of control, roaring like a beast.

And then I suddenly stopped. And blinked. And saw both Wilburs in their boxers. Their jeans were tied around their necks.

The girls stared openmouthed. I guess they couldn't believe what they'd just seen.

I couldn't believe it either.

And there was more to come.

I felt it rushing up my throat like a raging river. A fountain of black ink. I opened my mouth and it came spewing out of me.

The ink roared from my mouth and splashed over the Wilburs. I couldn't stop it. It poured over the two helpless boys, covering them in thick, gooey gunk.

"Help! Stop it!"

"Stop!"

They started to gasp and choke. They couldn't breathe.

Finally, the ink stopped spewing. I spit the last few drops onto the ground. The Wilburs were screaming and crying.

One of the girls turned to me. "Awesome magic trick!" she said.

But I backed away in horror.

I knew it wasn't my magic. It was evil magic. It was magic from the *thing* living inside me.

I had no control. No control of my own body.

What would Inkweed do next? What would happen to me next?

I turned toward my house and let out a scream: *"Oh no!"*

14

BUSTER!

My huge furry dog came running across the yard toward me, snarling and snapping his teeth.

Buster is a wolfhound. He's as big as a horse—and he *hates* me! Don't ask me why, because I don't know why. He just does.

"*Yaaaaiii!*" I let out a cry as the monster dog leaped at me. He knocked me to the ground with his powerful front paws and snapped his teeth at me, growling and snarling.

Buster liked to show me who was boss. Even though I didn't need to be told!

But this time, the furry beast was in for a surprise.

Once again, I felt the hot rage swell in my chest. It rose to my throat—and burst out of me in an ear-shattering scream of rage.

I lost control. My front yard became a swirling red blur.

Inkweed, with all his terrible rage, took over my body.

Without even realizing what I was doing, I grabbed Buster by his neck and stomach. I hoisted him off the ground.

He uttered a startled *yelp*.

I raised the huge dog high over my head and held him there as if he weighed nothing!

I let out another cry of rage—in a voice that wasn't mine, a voice I'd never heard before.

Then I raised the dog higher, tightened my muscles, and prepared to slam him to the ground.

The front door opened. Mom poked her head out. "Maxie?" she called. "You're playing with Buster? That's so *cute*! Don't move. I'm going to get the camera."

Mom vanished into the house.

I felt my muscles suddenly relax. With a loud sigh, I set Buster down gently on the grass. The confused dog stared up at me for a long moment. He made soft whimpering sounds. Then he turned and hurried away.

Dinner. Dad brought home a bucket of chicken, mashed potatoes, and cole slaw. A feast—but I didn't feel much like eating.

When Mom and Dad weren't looking, Colin shoved a wet gob of mashed potatoes into my T-shirt pocket. I just left it there. I didn't feel like getting into anything with Colin tonight.

I yawned. I kept blinking, trying to keep my tired eyes open.

Mom buttered a biscuit and took a bite. "Max, I almost forgot," she said. "Coach Freeley called, looking for you. He said your tryout for the swim team is tomorrow after school."

I nearly choked on my chicken leg. "Uh . . . I might be too tired to swim tomorrow. I haven't been sleeping well."

Dad had his plate piled high with chicken breasts and a mountain of mashed potatoes. He burped. Swallowed. Stared harshly at me. "Too tired? What kind of excuse is that?"

"A *lame* excuse?" Colin chimed in.

"Go to bed early tonight," Dad said. "You'll be ready to swim tomorrow."

I sighed. "Maybe this swim team thing is a bad idea," I said. "You know cold water makes my skin pucker up."

Dad slammed his fist on the table. One of his chicken breasts flew into his lap. "You're trying out tomorrow," he boomed. "You promised."

"Maybe I'll work out for a year or two first," I said. "You know. Get in shape. Then try out."

Dad glared at me. "You're going to make the team tomorrow, Max," he said. "Colin is a champion swimmer, and you will be too."

Colin jumped to his feet. "Would you like to see

57

all my trophies and medals, Max? Maybe that will inspire you."

"Sit down, Colin," Mom scolded. "You just want to show off."

"At least I have something to show off," Colin said. "Tell you what, Max. I'll inflate your floaties for you. You know you can't go in the water without them."

I was too sleepy to answer him.

Mom did it for me. "Colin, why do you always put your brother down?"

Colin shrugged. "Because it's *fun*?"

He poked me hard in the ribs with a chicken leg. I was so tired, I barely felt it.

Mom and Dad were talking about the swim team. I heard Dad say something about Coach Freeley and how important it was to bring my phys ed grade up.

But their voices faded into the distance. My eyelids felt heavier . . . heavier . . . too heavy to hold up.

I heard rain outside. Rain drumming against the kitchen window.

Their voices became water lapping . . . gentle waves brushing the shore.

Rushhhh . . . rushhhhhhh . . . rushhhhh . . . A soft sound in my ears.

My head slumped onto my dinner plate. A heavy darkness washed over me.

Rushhhh . . . rushhhhhhh . . . rushhhhh . . .

That gentle sound . . .

And then it, too, faded away. Silence now. And a deep darkness.

"Whoa!" I let out a shout as I felt myself being shaken roughly.

Colin! Colin had me by the shoulders and was shaking me awake.

He laughed. "Maxie fainted!" he exclaimed. "Did you see that, Dad? Little Maxie fainted because he's scared of trying out for the swim team!"

Dad laughed so hard that mashed potatoes came out his nose.

"Stop it, you two," Mom said, shaking her head. "Give Maxie a break."

Mom always sticks up for me. But Dad and Colin never pay attention.

Colin was showing Dad how my head had hit the mashed potatoes. They started laughing all over again.

I didn't care. I suddenly had an idea.

I thought I knew what Mr. Park, the old story-teller at the library, had been talking about.

"Uh . . . I have to make a phone call," I said. I jumped up from the table. I rushed to my room. I found Nicky and Tara doing ghost research at my computer.

"I think I've got it!" I cried. "I think I know what we have to do."

They both spun around. "Tell us," Tara said.

I yawned. How many hours had I been awake? I didn't want to count.

"Look outside," I said, pointing to my bedroom window. "It's raining real hard, right? No moon or stars."

"The darkest night," Nicky said.

"Yes," I agreed. "The darkest night. I think I know how to get rid of Inkweed!"

15

I SAT DOWN ON my desk chair. I propped my hands on my knees. I listened to the rain pattering against the window and struggled to think clearly.

"It's the darkest night," I repeated. "So we just have to find a place even darker."

"Yes!" Tara agreed, pumping her fists in the air. "You're right, Brainimon! You've figured it out."

Then Nicky said something. And Tara said something else.

I heard the raindrops hit the windowpane. And I heard *rushhhh ... rushhhhhhh ... rushh-hhh ...*

Dark now. The darkest night. I felt the darkness wrap around me.

Voices somewhere in the room. But far, far away. And the rush of water against the shore.

Then a deep silence.

"Huh?" I was awakened by someone shaking me again. This time it was Nicky.

His eyes were wide with fright. Tara stood next to him, shouting my name over and over.

I glanced down. A puddle of black ink had spread over my rug. My face felt wet. I rubbed it and stared at the black ink that had come off onto my hand.

"A close one," Nicky said, sighing. "We couldn't get you awake."

"Inkweed started to pour out," Tara said, shivering. "It was so awful." She squeezed my hand. "Hang on, Max. Please. You've *got* to hang on—or all three of us are doomed."

"Okay," I said, climbing shakily to my feet. "We have to act fast. I keep dozing off. I can feel him inside me. He's desperate to get out."

"We have to test your idea," Tara said.

"Yes." I crossed the room and clicked off the lights. I closed my bedroom door. The only light came from the computer monitor. I shut it off too.

Now the room was pitch black. So dark I couldn't see Nicky and Tara standing next to me.

"Come on, guys," I whispered. "Into the closet."

The darkest place on the darkest night.

My heart started to pound. I led them into my clothes closet. Even blacker in there than in my room.

They slipped in beside me. I pulled the door shut.

I settled back against a pile of T-shirts.

"This is dark," Nicky said. "Wow. It can't get any darker."

"It's so dark, I can't tell if my eyes are open or closed," I said.

"Just make sure they're *open*!" Tara said, giving me a shove.

"Okay. Everybody, take a deep breath," I whispered. "I think we've done what Mr. Park said to do. We're in the darkest place on the darkest night."

"It has to work," Tara whispered. "It *has* to!"

16

I LEANED AGAINST THE shirts and struggled to keep my eyes open.

No one said a word.

We waited . . . waited. Alert. Watching for a sign that the plan was working.

I felt Inkweed slide around behind my forehead. I felt him pressing the backs of my eyes.

Silence.

More time passed.

I started to count silently to myself. Slowly. Steadily. When I reached one hundred, I let out a long sigh.

"It isn't working," I said. I slammed my fist against the closet wall. "Something is wrong. Let's get out of here."

I pushed open the closet door. Nicky and Tara followed me into the room. I clicked on the ceiling light.

"How can it get any darker?" Nicky asked, scratching his head.

Tara tugged at her long red plastic earrings.

She did that whenever she was tense or afraid. She stared at me. "Did you feel anything, Max? Did you feel Inkweed start to come out?"

I shook my head. "He's in there," I said, tapping my forehead. "The dark closet didn't do anything to him."

"We need something even darker," Nicky said. He started to pace the room. "What could be darker than a closet?"

Rain pattered against the window. I knew this had to be the darkest night. We had that part right. We just didn't have the darkest place.

"How about the basement?" Tara asked.

Nicky stopped pacing. "Yes! The basement is even darker," he said.

"Okay. Good idea," I whispered.

I tiptoed out into the hall. My parents were watching TV in their bedroom. Colin was in his room playing a video game.

We made our way silently down to the basement. I turned off all the lights. We stepped into a corner where there were no windows.

"This is darker," I said. "This *has* to work."

I settled into an old armchair my dad planned to throw out. Nicky and Tara floated onto the chair arms.

"Max, do you feel anything?" Tara whispered.

"Not yet," I whispered back. "Don't talk anymore. Just wait."

65

I stared into the blackness. It was cold down there. I heard the *drip drip drip* of water in the sink in the laundry room at the other side of the basement. The only sound.

We waited . . . waited.

And once again, I started to drift into sleep. I couldn't help it. I couldn't tell where the darkness ended and I began. I couldn't tell if my eyes were open or shut.

My head fell forward. I started to sleep.

A noise startled me awake. I jumped up with a cry. I raised my eyes in time to see the basement door swing open at the top of the stairs. Light poured over us.

Dad appeared on the landing. He had his bathrobe on and a beer bottle in one hand. "Max? Is that you down there?" he bellowed.

"Uh . . . yeah," I managed to reply.

He squinted down at me. "It's late. What in blazes are you doing down there?" he boomed.

"Uh . . . well . . ."

Think fast, Max. Think fast.

"I'm doing dry laps, Dad," I said. "You know. Practicing my strokes. Getting ready for the swim team tryout tomorrow."

Would he buy that excuse? I held my breath.

"I'm impressed," he called down. "Keep up the good work, guy!" He slammed the basement door shut.

Darkness washed over us again. But not dark enough. The basement wasn't working either.

Settling back into the armchair, I turned to Nicky and Tara. "Are you still here?" I whispered. "Something is wrong. We haven't figured it out yet."

No reply.

"Nicky? Tara?"

They had disappeared again.

Bad timing. I really needed them now. Needed them to help me think. To help me . . . stay . . . awake . . . awake. . . . Can't stay . . . awake. . . . Can't do it . . . any longer. . . .

Darkness. Followed by deeper darkness.

I felt the ink pouring from my nose, from my mouth. Felt the warm black liquid seep out through my skin, drip by drip through my pores.

But I was helpless to do anything about it.

My head drooped as the evil ghost made his escape.

I could feel the liquid rush from my ears. Feel it ooze over my arms, my shoulders, my neck.

And start to cover me. Start to roll over me, like a heavy black ocean wave.

Rushhhhhh. Rushhhhhhh. . . . Rushhhhhhhh.

17

"Aaaaagggh!"

I woke up choking. I couldn't breathe.

Clots of ink clogged my throat. My face was covered. The ink poured over my hair.

"Nooooo!" Gagging, choking, I forced my throat clear.

Thrashing my arms, I pulled the heavy, wet shadow off me.

"Get off! Get off! Get off!" I screamed wildly. Kicking and thrashing at the sliding, shifting wet figure that had tried to smother me.

"Get off! Get *off!*"

I was wide awake now, breathing so hard, my sides ached.

Was I too late? How long had I slept? Long enough for Inkweed to make his escape?

No. As I screamed and thrashed, battling the wet, inky figure, it started to retreat. It grew smaller . . . smaller . . . oozing back into my skin.

And then it was gone again. Back inside me.

68

Slithering behind my forehead, shifting around my bones.

Inkweed had nearly escaped. He had tried to choke me, to smother me. And had failed. *This* time.

But what about *next* time?

I still didn't know how to defeat him.

There was only one thing I *did* know. I couldn't stay awake much longer.

Breakfast the next morning. Mom asked if I'd like eggs with my cereal or just cereal.

"Muhhhhhh mwwwwwwhhh," I answered.

I'd been up all night playing video games with Nicky and Tara. That meant I'd been awake for almost forty-eight hours.

Ever see any of those zombie movies with people staggering around like the living dead? That was me.

"Was that a yes or a no on the eggs?" Mom asked.

"Mwwwwww wwwwwmmmmm," I said. I didn't have the strength to open my lips.

I walked to school. A bright, sunny day, but I hardly noticed. I couldn't lift my head high enough to see the sky.

My backpack weighed about two tons. My *clothing* felt heavy!

Traci Wayne waved to me as she came out of

her house. Normally, this would be a thrill that I would think about for the rest of the day.

Traci Wayne waved to me!

Today, I muttered, "Mwwww muuuwwwww," and kept walking.

I dragged myself to class and slumped into my seat. I was so weak from no sleep, two kids had to help me pull off my backpack.

"Max, what's your problem?" Aaron asked.

"Muhhhhh wuhhhh," I told him.

He nodded as if he understood me. He's such a weird kid.

"I have a special announcement," Ms. McDonald said. I knew she was standing next to her desk at the front of the class. But I couldn't see that far. It was all just a fuzzy blur.

"We're having an assembly this morning," Ms. McDonald said. "I know you will all enjoy our speaker. Mr. Rudolph is an important businessman in our town."

Some kids groaned. I tried to groan, but nothing would come out.

Ms. McDonald ignored the groans. "Mr. Rudolph makes fire hydrants," she continued. "And he's come to our school this morning to explain to us how they work."

"Oh no!" a voice said in my ear.

I turned to see Nicky and Tara huddled next to me.

"Does this sound like the most boring assembly in school history?" Nicky said.

"Even more boring than the woman who explained how to recycle paper cups," Tara said.

They both stared hard at me. "Max will never stay awake through this assembly," Tara said to Nicky. "What are we going to do?"

18

WE FOLLOWED MS. MCDONALD into the auditorium. We were the first class there, so she marched us to the front. I found myself sitting in the second row.

A balding man with a bushy brown mustache sat on a folding chair onstage next to Mrs. Wright, our principal. The man wore a gray suit and a bright red necktie, which he kept nervously rolling and unrolling as he talked to Mrs. Wright.

The other classes poured in and filled the auditorium. Kids were laughing and complaining about how boring the assembly was going to be.

The Wilbur brothers sat on the other side of the aisle from me. They were already pretending to be asleep. They had their feet up on the seats in front of them and were snoring their heads off.

I settled back in my chair. I felt my eyelids start to droop.

"Don't go to sleep!" Nicky and Tara both screamed in my ear.

I jumped, blinking my eyes open.

Mrs. Wright stood behind the podium. The microphone squealed and shrieked. It took a while to fix.

"We have a very interesting guest today," Mrs. Wright said, smiling at Mr. Rudolph. He fiddled with his necktie while the principal introduced him.

"Let's give Mr. Rudolph a Jefferson School welcome!" Mrs. Wright said.

Some kids clapped politely.

Mr. Rudolph took the podium. He cleared his throat and started to speak in a high, soft voice. "I was fascinated by fire hydrants even when I was a kid," he said. "I used to take pictures of them, and study them, and sit on them. And when I was *really* little, I used to talk to them."

I wasn't sure if that was a joke or not. But a lot of kids laughed.

"Now I feel so lucky to be part of the fire hydrant family," Mr. Rudolph said. "Perhaps you kids don't know this. But there are actually six different kinds of fire hydrants."

My eyes shut. Mr. Rudolph's voice faded into the distance.

I guess I fell asleep.

I woke up laughing. "Ha, ha! Ha! Ho!"

Ow. A pain in my side. I turned to see Nicky and Tara tickling me.

Mr. Rudolph peered down at me from the stage. "Something funny, young man?" he asked.

I shook my head.

He pointed to a slide on the screen and continued his talk. "Now, here is my favorite hydrant," he said. "It's practical, it's long-lasting, and it's beautiful in an industrial sort of way. I like the curves of it, and . . ."

His voice faded again. I fell asleep.

"*Yaii!* Ha ha hahaha!" I woke up. My ghost friends were tickling me again.

Mr. Rudolph stopped speaking. He glared at me. "Do you find fire hydrants *funny?*" he asked. "I think they're very serious. Is there a joke I'm missing?"

"Hahaha. No," I said. "Stop tickling me! Ha ha ho ho ha!" I'm very ticklish.

Mrs. Wright jumped up from her seat beside the podium. "Let's be polite, Max," she scolded. "Mr. Rudolph has a lot to tell us."

"Fire hydrants can save your life," Mr. Rudolph continued, his eyes on me.

"You have to understand the whole system. And of course, you need to know about water pressure to understand the system. . . ."

His voice faded. I drifted off to sleep again.

"*Hahaha ha ha!* Stop it! *Stop it!*" I cried, jumping to my feet.

Nicky and Tara were tickling too hard.

Kids laughed and hooted and pointed at me.

Mrs. Wright leaped angrily to the podium. Her

face burned bright red. "Max, I'll have to ask you to leave," she snapped into the microphone.

"Ha ha ha," I said. I couldn't stop.

"Please apologize to our guest and leave the auditorium," the principal said, waving toward the doors at the back. "I'll see you in my office after school."

"Sorry," I muttered. Then I yawned. Really loudly.

More laughing and hooting all around me. As I pushed my way to the aisle and started to make the long walk to the exit at the back, kids cheered and clapped.

Not a great moment for Max Doyle. But I was too sleepy to even think about the trouble I was in.

I pushed open the door and staggered into the hall. I could hear Mr. Rudolph droning on behind me.

I yawned again. "Nicky? Tara? Are you here?" I asked.

Silence. No sign of them.

I leaned against the cool tile wall and tried to get myself together. My head weighed at least two tons. It took all my strength to keep my eyelids open.

I decided I'd go downstairs to the gym. Maybe work out a little.

I know. That wasn't like me at all. But I thought maybe exercise would help wake me up.

Blinking, yawning, I staggered to the stairs. I reached for the metal rail on the side—and missed.

I stumbled. And started to fall.

"Nooooo!" I let out a long howl as I tumbled all the way down the steep stairs, rolling over and over.

19

"Unnnnnh."

Was I hurt?

No. I'd landed flat on my back on something soft.

I heard someone groan. The sound seemed to come from *beneath* me.

I tried to roll off. But my arms and legs wouldn't cooperate. It took three tries.

I rolled away and pulled myself to my knees.

"Traci!" I cried out. She lay flat on her stomach on the floor, her hair over her face.

"Traci!"

I'd landed on Traci Wayne.

She raised her head and turned her face to me.

And what was that chocolatey stuff all over her face?

She sat up. The chocolate goop oozed down the front of her sweater, too. She shook her head, dazed. Chocolate dripped from her perfect blond hair.

I saw the tray of chocolate pudding on the

floor next to her. She'd been carrying the pudding cups. And then I fell on her. And now there was pudding all over her.

Did I want to die? Or disappear into the floor? Or both?

Of course. Do you have any idea how totally embarrassing it is to have a huge crush on a girl—and then fall down the stairs on her when she's carrying chocolate pudding cups?

Yikes.

Traci slowly climbed to her feet. She tried wiping the pudding off her sweater with both hands. But of course, that only got pudding all over her hands, too.

"Sorry about that," I muttered.

She frowned at me. "Max," she said, "this didn't really happen—*did* it?"

I swallowed. "I think it's real. I don't think we're dreaming."

She pulled a blob of pudding off her forehead. Then she said something totally shocking. "Max, do you promise not to fall on me if I come to your house tonight?"

Traci? Come to my house?

Of course, I realized what that meant. She wanted me to do her homework for her.

"N-no problem," I stammered.

But of course, there *was* a problem. A big problem. I'd already been awake for forty-eight hours.

How would I stay awake long enough to do Traci's homework?

And here was an even bigger problem. I'd just remembered my tryout for the swim team. It was after school.

How could I make the team if I was sound asleep in the water?

20

AFTER MY LAST CLASS, I dragged myself to the school's new pool and changed into my swimsuit. It took me a long moment to realize I'd put it on backward. I could barely see straight.

Coach Freeley greeted me at the edge of the pool. I nearly walked right into him!

The coach is built like a tank. He's very short and very wide, with bulging muscles everywhere you can have muscles. He has a broad chest that stretches his T-shirts tight over his perfect abs. He's young, and the girls all think he's really hot because of his wavy black hair and white-toothed smile.

He's a nice guy. He's always been nice to me. It was especially great of him to give me this special tryout.

If only I wasn't asleep on my feet!

"Take it easy at first, Max," he said. "Do some laps. Any kind of stroke you want. Just to warm up."

"Okay," I said. I hoped he didn't see my yawn.

I tried to dive in, but I fell off the edge. I landed with a *splat* on the surface of the water.

Brrr. They keep it pretty cold. Lucky for me. I thought it might wake me up.

I started with a simple breaststroke. I swam smoothly and with a steady rhythm.

I knew Coach Freeley was watching. I thought I was doing a good job, until—*clonnnk*—I bumped my head on the side of the pool.

Shaking it off, I turned in the water and tried my sidestroke. But my arms felt heavy. I didn't have the strength to kick. Too tired . . . too sleepy . . .

I felt myself sink under the surface.

Too sleepy . . .

I couldn't move my arms, my legs. Too tired and weak.

I shut my eyes and sank lower . . . lower.

From somewhere far away, I heard a splash. Soon after, two hands grabbed my waist. I opened my eyes and saw Nicky swimming beside me. He pulled me to the surface.

"Saved your life, Max."

I raised my head and took one deep breath, then another.

Nicky floated me to the side of the pool. Coach Freeley stood there watching me and shaking his head.

"I never had a swimmer *sink* before!" he said.

"But—" I started.

"You sank like a rock," the coach said. "What made you think you could be on the swim team? Did you think we have a hit-the-bottom-first competition?"

"But . . . ," I said.

"See you in gym class, Max," Coach Freeley said. "At least you can't sink in the gym!"

Still shaking his head, he started toward the locker room.

I turned to Nicky. Tara appeared beside him, treading water. "What am I going to do?" I wailed. "My dad will *kill* me! He'll never let me forget it if I don't make the swim team."

"Max, call to him," Tara said. "Tell him that's just your way of warming up."

"Yeah," Nicky said. "Ask for a second chance."

"Coach—come back!" I shouted. My hoarse voice echoed off the high tile walls. "That's just the way I warm up."

He stepped up to the pool edge. "You warm up by *drowning*?"

I nodded. "It helps my breath control. Please— give me a second chance," I pleaded.

He stared down at me. "Promise you won't sink to the bottom?"

"You'll be impressed," I said. "Really."

He crossed his massive arms in front of his

massive chest. "Go ahead, Max. Show me what you've got."

Of course, I didn't have *anything*. I could barely keep my head above water.

But Nicky and Tara went to work and made me look like an Olympic champion. The coach blew his whistle, and they each grabbed one side and rocketed me through the water. They shot me from end to end so fast, we sent up high waves on both sides. I looked like a torpedo!

I set the school speed record. I'm sure of it. Pretty good, considering I'd never even moved my arms or legs!

When I finished and floated over to the side of the pool, I was gasping for breath even though I hadn't moved a muscle.

Coach Freeley's whistle had fallen to his chest. His eyes bulged. He stared at me openmouthed. "Max, I think I'm gonna try that *sinking* warm-up with the rest of the guys!" he said. "You're fast. You're real fast!"

"Oh, I can do better than that," I said.

Nicky and Tara rolled their eyes.

"You made the team, buddy," the coach said, grinning at me. "I want you to demonstrate that stroke to everyone. I like how you keep your arms and legs close together and barely move them. Very aerodynamic. Super! Just super!"

"Thanks, coach," I said.

"Go get dried off. You're gonna be a star, Max." He turned and hurried away, his sneakers slapping the tiles.

"A star," I repeated, yawning. "A star . . ."

Nicky and Tara dragged me from the water. "I'm sleepwalking," I said. "I'm a real zombie. Not a pretend zombie."

"But you made the swim team," Nicky said.

I sighed. "I nearly drowned."

"Max, don't worry," Tara said, handing me a towel. "Nicky and I have a plan."

"Yeah. We've figured out what the old storyteller was telling us," Nicky said.

A smile spread over Tara's face. "We'll have you free of Inkweed tonight!" she said.

21

SO THIS IS WHERE we came in. Here we are, back at the beginning.

I'm sitting across my kitchen table from Traci Wayne. She's thumbing through a *Teen People* magazine, and I'm trying to do her homework for her.

That's not easy when your eyes keep closing and you just want to lay your head on the table and sleep.

"Max, do you have to yawn so loud?"

"Sorry, Traci."

Yawn, yawn.

She grabbed my wrist. "Max, you're trying to write with the eraser side of the pencil," she said. "Use the *lead* side."

"Oh. Yeah," I murmured. My eyes were so tired, I couldn't see one end of the pencil from the other.

"You're a real clown tonight," Traci said. "How come you're in such a jokey mood, Max?"

"Ha, ha," I said. I couldn't think of a better answer.

I climbed to my feet. "I have to go up to my room and get my calculator," I said. "I'll be right back."

She didn't look up from her magazine.

Do you believe it? Traci Wayne was actually in my house, sitting across from me. And all I wanted to do was sleep. How bizarre was that?

Going to my room was a big mistake.

I started toward the desk to get my calculator. But I couldn't keep my eyes off my bed. It appeared to have a glowing light around it. And I heard a choir of angelic voices calling to me, calling me to the glowing bed.

I tried to fight it. But the bed pulled me like a strong magnet.

Before I realized it, I was curled up on top of the covers.

Just a short nap, I told myself. Just a few seconds. Nothing bad can happen in a few seconds.

I shut my eyes. I felt Inkweed stir inside me. I could feel him tense and grow alert.

Nicky came to the rescue again. I woke up with a gasp. He was shaking me by the shoulders. "No sleeping, Max," he said. "Snap out of it."

Blinking, I saw ink stains all over my bedspread.

"Just a few more hours to go," Tara said,

somewhere behind him. "A few short hours, and you'll be free."

Nicky pulled me to the stairs. "Wake up, Max. Go finish Traci's homework. Then we can see about dealing with Inkweed."

"Yes. Homework," I muttered. My eyes were closed. I didn't see the first step.

My foot missed and I started to fall.

"Heyyyyy!" I cried out in shock as I went tumbling down the stairs.

I landed at the bottom on something soft.

Traci!

"That's it! I'm *outta* here!" she cried.

"But, Tracy—"

She scrambled to her feet. "I warned you not to fall on me again, Max. How many times a day do you think you can fall on me?"

"Two?" I replied.

She let out a growl. Then, her blond hair flying behind her, she quickly gathered up all her books and papers. She stuffed them into her backpack and ran out of the house. The front door slammed hard behind her.

I picked myself up from the floor and tested my arms and legs to make sure I hadn't broken anything. I was still stretching and bending when my mom stepped into the room.

"Traci left so soon?" she asked.

I nodded. "Yeah."

"How was the study date?" Mom asked. "Did you help her?"

"Oh, sure," I said. "I did those problems with my eyes shut."

"Don't brag, Max," Mom said.

"Good night," I said. I hurried back to my room. Nicky and Tara were waiting there. "Are you ready?" I asked. "Do you really think you can get rid of Inkweed so I can go to sleep?"

"No problem," Nicky said.

"No problem," Tara echoed. "We've got it all figured out."

22

WE HAD TO WAIT till my parents were asleep. Then I put on a jacket and we silently sneaked out of the house.

It was a cool, windy night. The bushes and trees all shivered and shook. The cold air helped refresh me.

We walked for miles, keeping in the shadows, darting through front yards. We hid whenever we saw the headlights of a car approaching.

"What are we doing?" I asked. "Where are we?"

I didn't recognize the neighborhood. We had passed all the houses. Squinting into the darkness, now I could see only woods and fields.

Nicky grabbed my shoulder. "Look up," he said. He tilted my head upward.

I gazed into the black sky. "I don't see anything," I said.

"That's the point," Tara said. "No stars, no moon. This is the darkest night of the month. No moon tonight."

"The darkest night," I muttered. "Do you think this is what the old storyteller meant?"

"Could be," Tara replied.

"And where are you taking me?" I asked again.

They both pointed to a small sign attached to a wooden fence post. I had to move closer to read the sign.

DARK CAVERNS.

"I remember these caverns from a field trip we took in second grade," Tara said.

I stared past the fence. But I could see only the shape of black hills against an even blacker sky.

The wind fluttered my jacket. I zipped the zipper all the way to the collar. "What's so special about them?" I asked.

"They're supposed to be the deepest, darkest caverns in the country," Tara said.

I stared at her. "You want me to climb into caverns?" I cried. "You know I'm allergic to caverns. They're dark and cold and . . . and . . . and they make me sneeze." I held my nose. "I . . . I'm starting to sneeze already. Just being *close* to a cavern makes me sneeze!"

Nicky and Tara waited for me to stop ranting. Then Tara said, "Don't you see? It's the darkest place on the darkest night."

"It has to work," Nicky said, crossing his fingers on both hands. "It has to be right."

They both grabbed me and started pulling me toward the caverns.

In a few minutes, we stood in front of an enormous cave entrance. Cut into the side of a steep hill, it rose high above our heads. A deep, black hole, blacker than the night, blacker than the sky.

The darkest place on the darkest night.

Holding on to my shoulders, my two ghost friends pushed me into the cavern entrance.

"Uh . . . did anyone bring a flashlight?" I asked.

23

THE WIND STOPPED AS we stepped into the cavern opening. But the air grew colder.

The cold washed over me like a high ocean wave. I shivered and waited for my eyes to adjust to the darkness. But they *couldn't* adjust. I could see only different shades of black.

"Damp in here," Tara said, gripping my arm tighter. "It's kinda like walking into a refrigerator."

"Hope there aren't any bats," Nicky said in a whisper.

"Bats?" I said. "Why did you have to mention bats? Couldn't you keep that to yourself?"

Nicky snickered. "Hey! Woke you up!"

We walked side by side. The ground squished under my shoes, soft and muddy. We followed a narrow path that curved between two rock walls. The path sloped down sharply.

I felt my shoes slide in the mud. Nicky and Tara held me up.

"How far down do we have to go?" I asked.

My voice echoed all around, repeating my question again and again off the high cavern walls.

"Creepy," I said.

Creepy . . . creepy . . . creepy . . . came the cavern's echoing reply.

We walked in silence for a few minutes, edging our way slowly down. I could feel the mud ooze up over my ankles.

I stopped and gazed back. I hoped to see the sky, but the cavern entrance was no longer in view.

"What if we get lost in here?" I asked. "No one would ever find us."

"Max, stop scaring me," Tara said.

I gasped when I felt Inkweed stir inside my head. This time, he didn't slither. He felt like a strong breeze between my ears.

Did the evil ghost realize what we were doing? Did he know we were taking him to the darkest place on the darkest night?

Is that why I could feel him tense up inside me?

Did he realize we were about to destroy him?

I rubbed my nose. It was numb, totally frozen. My skin tingled from the damp cold. I looked down. I couldn't see my shoes.

"Isn't this dark enough?" I asked, my voice echoing all around. I lowered it to a whisper. "It can't get any blacker than this."

"Okay. Let's give it a try," Nicky said.

"Give *what* a try?" I asked. "What do we have to do?"

He sighed. "Just wait, I guess."

"Yeah. We're in the right place at the right time. So . . . we'll just wait until Inkweed dies," Tara said.

They guided me to a low, flat rock ledge at the edge of the path. I sat down and crossed my arms tightly in front of me, trying to warm up. My shoes tapped on the soft ground. I was so cold and nervous, I couldn't stop my legs from pumping up and down.

"Shhh. Be quiet, Max," Tara said. "Sit still. Give Inkweed a chance to come out and die."

I forced my legs to keep still. I took long deep breaths of the cold cave air.

I kept gazing around, even though I couldn't see a thing. The darkness was so heavy and thick, it was like being asleep while you're awake. Or in a dream where the whole world has disappeared.

Nicky and Tara stood beside me as I hunched on the edge of the rock ledge. We waited. And waited . . .

I heard a sound. A soft scraping. Growing louder.

Inkweed! Sliding out of me!

No.

The sound came from a distance.

94

I sat up straight, suddenly alert.

I heard a steady rhythm of scraping sounds. Soft thuds. Growing louder. Approaching fast.

Footsteps!

My heart thudding, I turned to Nicky and Tara. "We . . . we're not alone in here," I whispered.

24

PERCHED ON THE ROCK ledge, I hugged myself and listened. The footsteps were soft, muffled, as if someone was trying not to be heard.

"Nicky? Tara? Do you hear it?" I whispered. "What should we do?"

Silence.

The soft thuds came closer. Someone—or something—was slowly, carefully navigating the path down from the cavern entrance.

"Nicky? Tara?"

No reply.

They had disappeared.

How could they do that? How could they leave me here in this freezing, dark cave—all alone with someone approaching . . . someone very near now . . . very near?

"Nicky? Tara?"

Something bumped my ankle.

I cried out.

It pulled back fast.

I heard the scrape of several paws all around me.

Something swiped at my leg.

I started to jump up from the ledge. Before I could move, two eyes stared into mine.

And slowly, my eyes focused on the creature at my feet.

A fat raccoon.

It pawed my leg again.

"Go away," I said, panic choking my voice. "Beat it."

It didn't move.

I turned and saw another raccoon staring up at me. And another beside it, pawing at the side of my rock ledge.

Five or six raccoons came into view. They had formed a loose circle around me. One raised its front paws as if begging.

What did they want? Did they expect me to feed them?

They're rabid! I suddenly thought. They're planning to attack!

Another raccoon raised its front paws and stared at me. Beside him, a fat one scraped the rock ledge with its claws.

Their circle grew tighter.

I took a deep breath. *"Go away!"* I shouted. *"I'm not kidding! Go away!"*

My voice boomed through the cavern. It

echoed and bounced off the cavern walls until the words were lost in a jumble of noise.

I jumped to my feet. *"Scat! Scat!"*

To my surprise, they turned and took off. Their paws slapped the mud as the entire pack ran up the path toward the entrance.

Breathing hard, I slumped back onto the rock ledge.

"Nicky? Tara?"

No. They still weren't back.

I shut my eyes and tried to force my heartbeats back to normal. I shivered. I'd never been so cold. Or alone. Or frightened.

Closing my eyes was a bad idea. I suddenly felt sleepy again.

I felt Inkweed slither around behind my forehead.

He was supposed to be dying. Taking him to this dark cavern was supposed to destroy him.

"It's sure taking a long time," I said out loud.

I yawned. "A very long time."

I felt the evil ghost push at the backs of my eyeballs.

Something is terribly wrong, I realized. It isn't working.

Unless I just have to wait longer . . . ?

But I couldn't wait here in this freezing cave much longer. I had to get out and see the sky again. See some light. In this deep blackness, I couldn't tell if my eyes were open or not.

The darkest place on the darkest night.

Well, here I am. And it's not working.

I yawned again. I could feel myself drifting, drifting into the darkness. I could feel it pulling me, deeper and deeper . . . into a deep sleep. . . .

And as I started to sleep, I felt my mouth open. And a laugh burst out—a hoarse, dry, *terrifying* laugh that made the cave walls roar.

Haa haaaaaaaaaaaah!

Inkweed's laugh!

Pouring from my open mouth. An evil, inhuman laugh. A laugh of victory.

Because Inkweed knew I couldn't last much longer. He knew I couldn't stay awake.

The darkness was pulling me . . . pulling me down into a deep sleep.

I couldn't fight it any longer. I stretched out on the flat rock ledge.

"Sorry, guys," I whispered to Nicky and Tara, just in case they could hear me. "I have to sleep. I'm sorry. I let you down. I'm sorry. . . ."

I curled up on the ledge, hugging myself for warmth.

But before I could close my eyes, a flash of bright light made me cry out. I struggled to a sitting position, blinking toward the light. And stared at two bright round eyes. Glowing yellow eyes floating rapidly toward me.

"Who—who are you?" I tried to scream, but my voice came out in a hoarse rasp.

"Who are you?" I tried again.

No answer.

The glowing yellow eyes shimmered like car headlights. They stared intensely at me as they floated closer. So bright, I covered my eyes with one hand.

"Who are you?" I found my voice and screamed now in my fright.

"What do you want? Who *are* you?"

25

I HEARD THE SCRAPE of footsteps. A murmured voice.

The eyes bobbed in the blackness, floating down from the cavern opening.

"Hello?" I called. "Please—answer me!"

I fought off my fear and jumped to my feet. I tensed my muscles, ready to run.

What kind of creature comes loping down into a cavern with glowing yellow eyes?

It had to be some kind of *monster*!

Had Inkweed summoned a friend?

Half covering my eyes from the blinding glare, I watched the creature move down the path toward me.

And then I heard whispered voices, talking rapidly. The two eyes moved apart. The lights raised, beamed up to the cavern ceiling for a moment, then soared back down.

And I saw two figures standing in front of me. Two people holding flashlights.

At first, I could see only their outlines behind the glowing circles of light. Arms and legs. And then the lights moved again.

And I cried out. "Mom! Dad! How did you find me?"

26

THEY LOWERED THEIR FLASHLIGHTS. "Max?" Mom called. "What are you doing here in the middle of the night?" Her voice echoed off the cavern walls.

"I—I—It's hard to explain," I stammered.

And then I ran to her, threw my arms around her, and hugged her.

"You're in a lot of trouble," Dad said.

I backed away from Mom. "You don't know the half of it," I said. "You don't know what horrible trouble I'm in."

"I need my sleep," Dad growled. "I *like* my sleep. I don't want to be crawling around in freezing cold, dark caves in the middle of the night."

I swallowed. "I know," I murmured. I didn't know what else to say. I was so happy to see them. But I could see Dad getting angrier and angrier, about to explode.

I turned to my mom, tiny and thin and birdlike. In the dim circle of light from her flashlight, I could see that she was trembling.

"Did you follow me here?" I asked her. "How did you know I was down here?"

A strange smile spread over Mom's face. "Do you think I couldn't find my own son?"

"You're in trouble, Max," Dad said, shaking his head. "You're in the biggest trouble of your life."

"Please—take me home," I said in a trembling voice. "Please—"

"Why don't you lie down on that rock?" Mom said, pointing with her light. "Lie down and go to sleep, Max."

"Huh?" I stared at her.

"It's the best thing," Dad said. "Go ahead, Max. Go to sleep. You need to sleep."

"But, I can't—" I started. "You don't understand. I—I—"

Mom lowered her voice to a whisper. "Go to sleep, Max. Let Inkweed pour out."

"Listen to your mother," Dad said. "Let Inkweed out, Max."

"I don't understand!" I cried. "How do you know about Inkweed?"

"We're your parents," Mom said. "We know everything about you."

"Go to sleep," Dad said again. "You're very sleepy, Max. Let Inkweed out. Let Inkweed *live*!"

My mouth dropped open, and a hoarse cry of shock escaped my throat.

They can't *be my parents!* I thought.

They can't *know about Inkweed! They* can't *want Inkweed out!*

I stared at them, trembling in horror, and watched them raise their flashlights under their chins. The light spilled over their faces with an eerie glow.

"Let Inkweed out. Let Inkweed out," they both chanted.

"Mom! Dad! Why are you doing this?" I cried.

They didn't answer. They opened their mouths wide.

I heard a gurgling. Then a horrifying *retching* sound from deep in their throats.

And then *gushers* of black ink spewed from their mouths.

I raised my hands to cover my face as it poured over me, hot and putrid. The twin streams of ink washed over my head, down my shoulders. I heard it splash at my feet.

My parents made ugly retching sounds, as if they were vomiting the hot, smelly ink from deep inside them. I couldn't move away from it. I struggled to breathe.

The black ink shot over me, splashing hard, pounding my head, dropping me to my knees.

I tried to breathe—and sucked ink into my nose, down my throat. Burning ink. It tasted sour, like spoiled milk.

I started to gag and choke.

I flailed my arms. I tried to dive away from it.

But the streams were too powerful. They covered me.

Covered me . . .

Covered me in a thick, sticky blanket of darkness.

I heard the retching sounds. The splash of ink on the cavern floor.

Then silence.

And a darkness that swallowed me whole . . .

27

I OPENED MY EYES to loud shouts in my ear. Startled, I realized I was standing up.

Nicky was shouting for me to wake up. He and Tara had me by the arms. They were walking me away, guiding me up the path.

My feet slid in the mud. I blinked my eyes and gazed around in confusion.

"Mom?"

"Dad?"

"No, it's us," Tara said. "Snap out of it, Max."

"But my mom and dad—" I choked out. "They were here. They told me to go to sleep and—"

"You must have been dreaming," Tara said. "Nicky and I popped back just in time."

I gazed up toward the cavern entrance. No bright lights. No Mom and Dad.

The dream had been so real, so terrifying.

"Wh-what happened?" I stammered. "Did Inkweed—?"

"We came back just in time," Nicky said. "We dragged you to your feet before Inkweed could get out."

"Sorry we left you here," Nicky said. "Sometimes we disappear. We can't control it."

"Are you okay?" Tara asked, helping me over a jagged rock.

I stopped.

"No," I said. "How could I be okay? We're in terrible trouble. Coming here didn't work. It didn't work at all."

Up ahead, I saw the gray of the sky. I could feel the damp, cold air fall away as we approached the entrance. "Inkweed is still inside me. I can feel him."

"Hang on, Max," Tara said as we stepped out through the cavern entrance. "Hang on."

Trees shivered all around in a strong breeze. Cool, dry air. I took several deep breaths. It smelled so good and clean.

"We'll figure this out. I know we will," Tara said.

Her voice trembled. I could hear how frightened she was now.

We had tried and failed. And we all knew I couldn't stay awake much longer.

As we walked, I tried to figure out how many hours I'd been awake. But my brain was too fuzzy to do the math.

Close to seventy hours. That was the best I could figure.

I kept walking with them. But I couldn't really feel my legs. It was as if they were moving on their own.

The trees spun around me. The ground tilted one way, then the other.

How long did we walk?

I don't know. It was a long walk home.

We were on a block with little houses hidden behind hedges and thick clumps of trees. Suddenly, Nicky and Tara stopped. Their grip tightened on my arms. They stared at the steeply sloping hill across the street.

"What's wrong?" I whispered.

"Look," Nicky said. "The library."

I squinted hard, trying to force my eyes to focus. "Library?"

"Mr. Park's library," Tara said. "Where we got the old book."

"The lights are on," Nicky said. "Do you think Mr. Park is awake?"

"If he isn't, we'll wake him up," Tara said. She pulled hard, dragging me up the sloping front yard. "He has to help us. Max, you'll tell him what we did tonight. The darkest place on the darkest night. You'll tell him it didn't work."

We stepped up to the little house. The lights were on in the front room.

Nicky pushed the doorbell. "He'll know what to do," he said. "He'll help us. I know he will."

28

NICKY PUSHED THE BELL again. I saw a shadow move in the front window.

The front door opened a crack. Someone peeked out.

"Hi, it's me," I said.

A chain slid off the door. The door opened wider, and I saw the storyteller's daughter, Sumner Park, squinting out at me. She wore a long purple bathrobe. Her hair was tied back.

"You're the boy who was here the other day?" she said.

I nodded. "Max Doyle. I need—"

"Max, what are you doing here in the middle of the night?" she asked. Of course, she couldn't see Nicky and Tara.

She stepped aside so I could come in. "It's nearly three in the morning. Do your parents know where you are?"

"Don't waste time answering her questions, Max," Tara said. "Tell her to wake up her dad."

"Okay," I said. "I'll do it."

"Do what?" Ms. Park asked.

"I need to see your dad," I said. "It's very important."

She studied me. "Look at your shoes. You're covered with mud. And you look so tired, Max. Something's wrong, isn't it. Let me call your parents."

She reached for the phone on her desk.

Tara grabbed it away.

Ms. Park gasped. "That phone! It's floating in midair!"

"I . . . uh . . . heard the phone bills are going *up*!" I said. "Guess it's true."

I grabbed the phone from Tara. "I don't want you to call my parents," I said to the librarian. "I just need to see your father."

"I'm sorry," Ms. Park said. "He's asleep. I should be asleep too. But I was busy arranging books, and I lost track of the time."

"We'll wake him," Tara said. She and Nicky went running to the stairs.

"No! You can't!" I shouted to them.

"Can't what? Max, you're not making any sense," Ms. Park said. "I really think we should call—"

"It—it's an emergency!" I stammered.

I ran after Nicky and Tara and followed them up the stairs.

"Hey! Come back!" Ms. Park shouted. "You

can't go up there! Come back here! Tell me what this is about! Come back here!"

I was halfway up the stairs. She came chasing after me, shouting for me to stop.

I reached the landing and followed Nicky and Tara down the hall. I was gasping for air by the time we stopped at Mr. Park's bedroom. The door was shut. I grabbed the knob and turned it.

"Stop right there," Ms. Park said sharply. "You can't go in, Max. My dad locks his door at night. No way are you going in."

I sighed. "The door is locked?"

She nodded. "And he's a very sound sleeper."

With a sad sigh, I turned to Nicky and Tara. "*Now* what are we going to do?"

29

"**WHO ARE YOU TALKING** to?" Ms. Park asked.

I stared at the locked bedroom door.

Tara tapped me on the shoulder. "Max, did you forget Nicky and I are ghosts?"

Before I could answer, the two of them floated right through the door, into Mr. Park's bedroom.

"Let's go downstairs, Max," Ms. Park said sternly. "I think you're in some kind of trouble. Come downstairs, and we can call your parents."

"I *am* in trouble," I told her. "But I think your dad can help me."

"Maybe tomorrow," she said. "I can't wake him up."

But we heard the lock snap on the other side of the door. And Mr. Park's bedroom door swung open.

"Come in, Max. Hurry," Tara said, pulling me through the doorway.

We ran to Mr. Park's bed. He was asleep on his back, the covers pulled up to his chin.

"How did you do that? How did you unlock

114

the door?" Sumner Park came running into the room after us. "You can't wake him," she said. "He sleeps so soundly."

"We'll wake him," Tara said. "Nicky. Hurry. Start tickling."

They pulled down the blankets, tugged up his red pajama shirt, and started tickling his ribs.

It only took a few seconds. Mr. Park started wiggling and squirming. And then he woke up, laughing.

"Dad!" Ms. Park cried in surprise. "What's so funny?"

He scratched at the curly white hair on top of his head. "Must have been having a funny dream." Then he saw me. "You? What are *you* doing here?"

"It's an emergency," I said. "I'm sorry to wake you. Really. But I really need your help."

Blinking himself awake, he pulled himself up. "My help?" He looked over my shoulder at his daughter. "Sumner, what is the problem here? How did he get in here? The door was locked."

Ms. Park shrugged. "I don't know, Dad. He was determined to see you."

He squinted at me with his bright blue eyes. "Max, right?"

"Yes," I said. "I—"

"What is the problem, Max?"

"It's about Inkweed," I said. "I didn't tell you

the whole truth the other day. You see, Inkweed is inside me."

He made a gulping sound. He scratched his head again.

"I did what you said," I told him, speaking breathlessly. "I went to a dark cavern. Tonight. A night when there is no moon."

He kept squinting at me. He looked as if he didn't understand what I was telling him.

"Don't you see? The darkest place on the darkest night? That's where you told me to go. But it didn't work, Mr. Park. It didn't work at all."

Mr. Park turned his body and lowered his feet to the floor. "Max, you wanted *real* advice?" he asked.

"Yes. Of course," I said. "I tried what you told me, but—"

"That was just a story," Mr. Park said.

My breath caught in my throat. "Huh?"

"It was just a story I made up," Mr. Park said. "It wasn't supposed to be real advice. The darkest place on the darkest night? I just made that up."

"I told you," his daughter said. "My dad is a storyteller. He makes up stories."

Mr. Park nodded. "I made up that story on the spot. I thought you enjoyed it."

"It—it wasn't real?" I gasped. I still couldn't believe it.

"Inkweed isn't real," Mr. Park said. "Inkweed

is a legend. A myth. A ghost story, like all the others."

"But—but—" I sputtered.

"There's no one like Dad," Ms. Park said. "He makes up the wildest stories. He can make up dozens of them in an afternoon. You should come hear him perform sometime, Max."

"Uh . . . yeah," I muttered.

I knew I couldn't convince them of the truth. I knew I couldn't convince them that Inkweed was real. And I was too tired to try.

"Come back sometime, Max, and I'll tell you some more Inkweed stories," Mr. Park said.

"Maybe I'll tell *you* some stories next time," I murmured.

If there's a next time.

30

NICKY AND TARA DRAGGED me home. I don't know how they did it. My legs wouldn't work at all. And I kept saying, "It wasn't real? It wasn't real?" again and again.

They carried me through the back door, into the kitchen. Tara flashed on a light. I dropped into a chair at the table, nearly unconscious.

"I'm sorry, guys," I croaked. "I . . . I can't stay awake another minute. I . . . I'm so sorry."

"Max, you've got to try!" Tara said. She held my head up off the kitchen table with both hands. "Try, Max. Give Nicky and me a chance to think up a new plan."

"No new plan," I muttered. The room spun in front of me. My head felt as if it weighed a thousand pounds. "No new plan. We lose. Inkweed wins. We lose. Lose. . . ."

My eyes started to close.

Tara held on to my head. "Open your eyes, Max. Come on. You can do it." She turned to

Nicky. "Turn on the TV. Maybe that will keep him awake."

"We lose," I murmured. "We lose."

I was out of my mind. I didn't know *what* I was saying.

Nicky clicked on the TV on the kitchen counter. I squinted across the room. I couldn't get my tired, burning eyes to focus.

It took me a while to realize I was watching a toilet paper commercial.

A woman was rubbing toilet paper against her face, saying how soft it was.

I watched her for a few seconds. Then I struggled to my feet.

"Nicky! Tara!" I cried. "We can do it. We can destroy Inkweed!"

31

THEY GAPED AT ME, their eyes wide. "We *can*?" Tara said.

"Toilet paper," I said. "Colin said Dad bought three cases of it. Hurry. Go down to the basement. Bring up a case."

They hesitated for a moment. Then they took off, shooting right through the basement door without opening it.

I pinched my cheeks hard while I waited for them to return. Pinched myself until it hurt. Anything to stay awake.

Finally, they returned, carrying a big plastic package filled with toilet paper rolls. "Open it," I said. "Hurry. I can't hold on much longer."

"Okay, it's open," Tara said. She had a roll of the white paper in each hand. "Now what, Max?"

"Now I go to sleep," I said. I put my head on the table and shut my eyes. "Good night, everyone."

I fell asleep in two seconds. Maybe faster. A deep sleep with no dreams.

Nicky and Tara told me later that as soon as I was asleep, Inkweed started to pour out.

Ink seeped out through my skin. Came oozing out in all his inky blackness, through my arms, my neck, my face, through my nose and mouth.

They stood watching in horror as the inky creature poured silently from my body. The ink formed a steaming black puddle on the floor beside my chair.

When it had all oozed out, it slowly slid off the floor. It raised itself onto the wall—and formed a man's shadowy figure.

"Get him! *Get* him!"

Tara's shouts woke me from my sleep. I jumped up, gasping, my heart thudding in my chest.

I saw Inkweed rising up on the kitchen wall. Pushing my chair away, I dove for the toilet paper rolls.

Without a word, Nicky, Tara, and I rushed at Inkweed. And we began wiping the toilet paper over him. Dabbing frantically, wiping hard, rubbing the inky figure.

"It's working!" I cried. "It . . . it's *absorbing* him!"

Inkweed tried to dodge away. His wet, inky body slid one way, then the other against the wall.

But the two ghosts and I had him trapped.

I dove to the carton and tossed Nicky and Tara

more rolls. Then I leaped back to the wall and wiped furiously, wiped a whole roll against Inkweed's chest. Absorbing him . . . absorbing the hot, smelly ink.

We pressed roll after roll against him. The black ink soaked into the paper quickly.

We had to keep diving to the package and tossing more rolls to each other.

Inkweed squirmed and thrashed, ducked and dodged. But he couldn't escape.

We soaked him up. He never made a sound.

It took two dozen rolls. But the wall was clean. No ink. No Inkweed!

Gasping for breath, Nicky, Tara, and I dropped to the kitchen floor. I gazed around. The floor was littered with ink-soaked toilet paper rolls. I had ink all over my hands, my arms, my clothes.

"We . . . did it," I choked out in a breathless whisper.

"We absorbed him," Tara said. She raised her hand to slap me a high five. But I was too weary to slap back.

I heard the ceiling creak above me.

"Uh-oh," I said. "Someone is moving around upstairs."

I jumped to my feet. "Quick. Help me carry all this toilet paper to the trash cans behind the garage."

We tossed the inky rolls into a garbage bag and dragged it out to the back. Then I slumped into the kitchen, yawning.

"You saved our lives, Max!" Tara declared. "I'm so proud of you. You did it. You really did it."

To my surprise, she threw her arms around me and gave me a hug that almost knocked me over.

"Yeah, thanks, dude," Nicky said after Tara backed away. "We owe you one. Big-time."

"You can thank me some more in the morning," I said, yawning. "I'm going to bed now. And I'm going to sleep for hours and hours and hours."

I started toward the kitchen doorway, and Mom burst through it in her bathrobe. "Max!" she cried. "You're up early!"

"Yeah. Well—" I started.

"And you're already dressed. Great!" Mom exclaimed. "Here. Take these eggs. Get some milk. You can help me make breakfast."

She smiled at me. "Big day in school today? Is that why you're up so early?"

For the first time in my life, I didn't have an answer.

ABOUT THE AUTHOR

Robert Lawrence Stine's scary stories have made him one of the bestselling children's authors in history. "Kids like to be scared!" he says, and he has proved it by selling more than 300 million books. R.L. teamed up with Parachute Press to create Fear Street, the first and number one bestselling young adult horror series. He then went on to launch Goosebumps, the creepy bestselling series that gave kids chills all over the world and made him the number one children's author of all time (*The Guinness Book of Records*).

R.L. Stine lives in Manhattan with his wife, Jane, their son, Matthew, and their dog, Nadine. He says he has never seen a ghost—but he's still looking!